I am a t ?

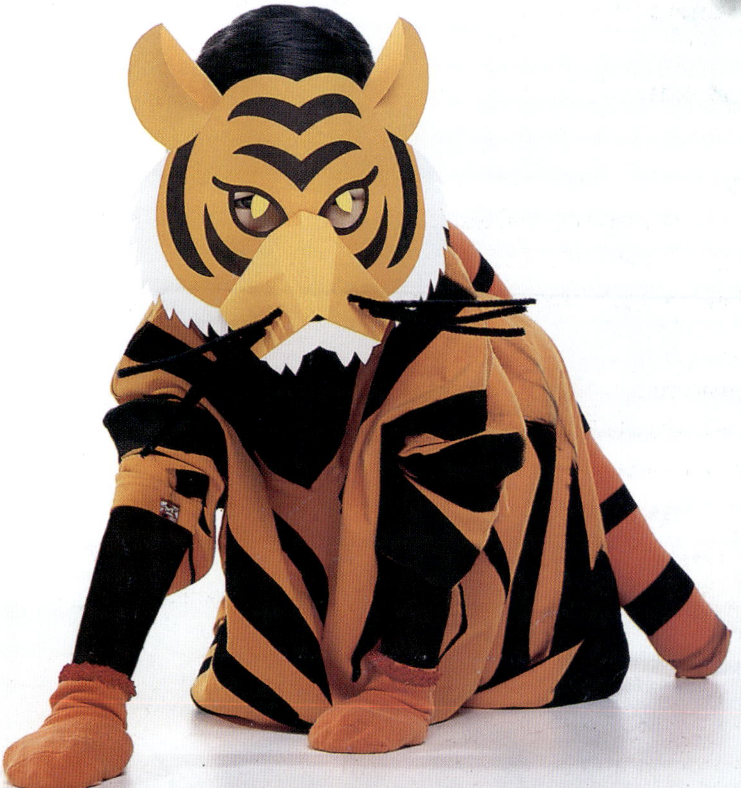

Look at my eyes.

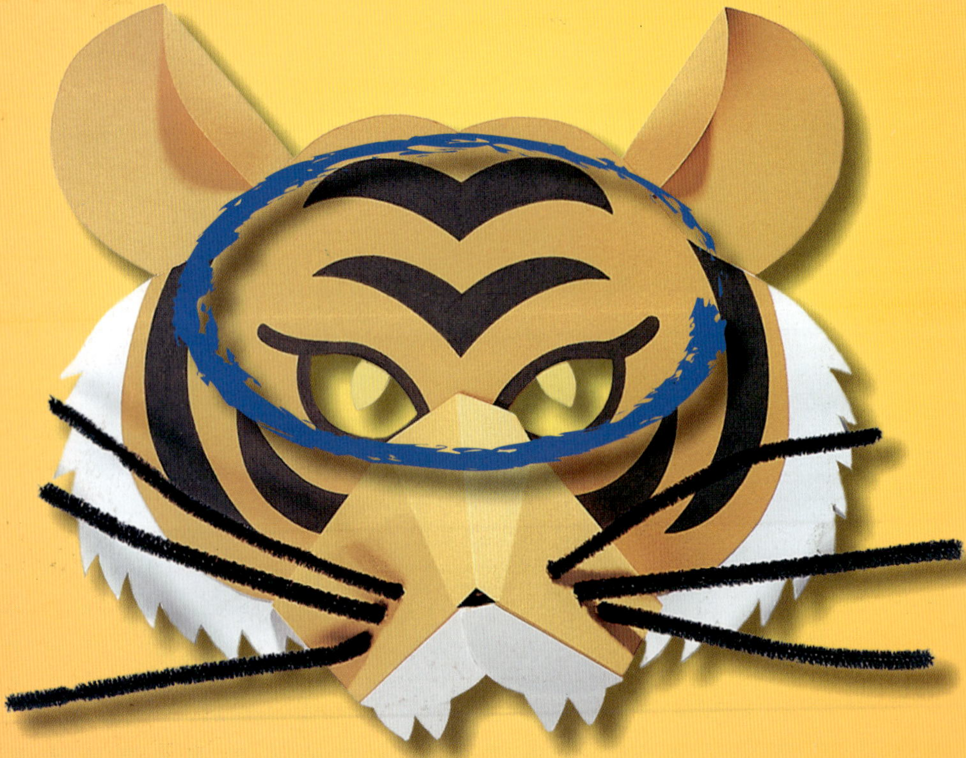

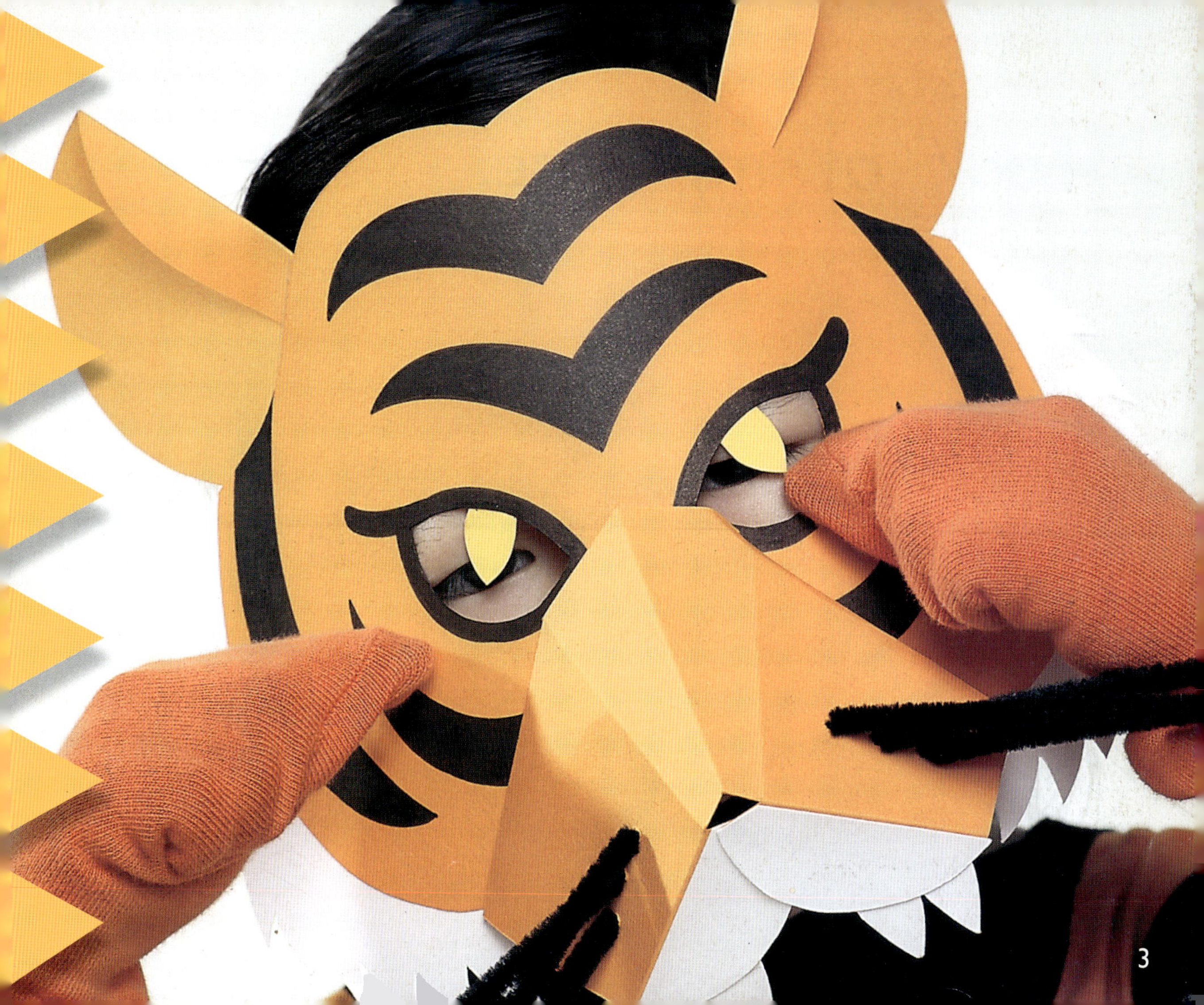

Look at my nose.

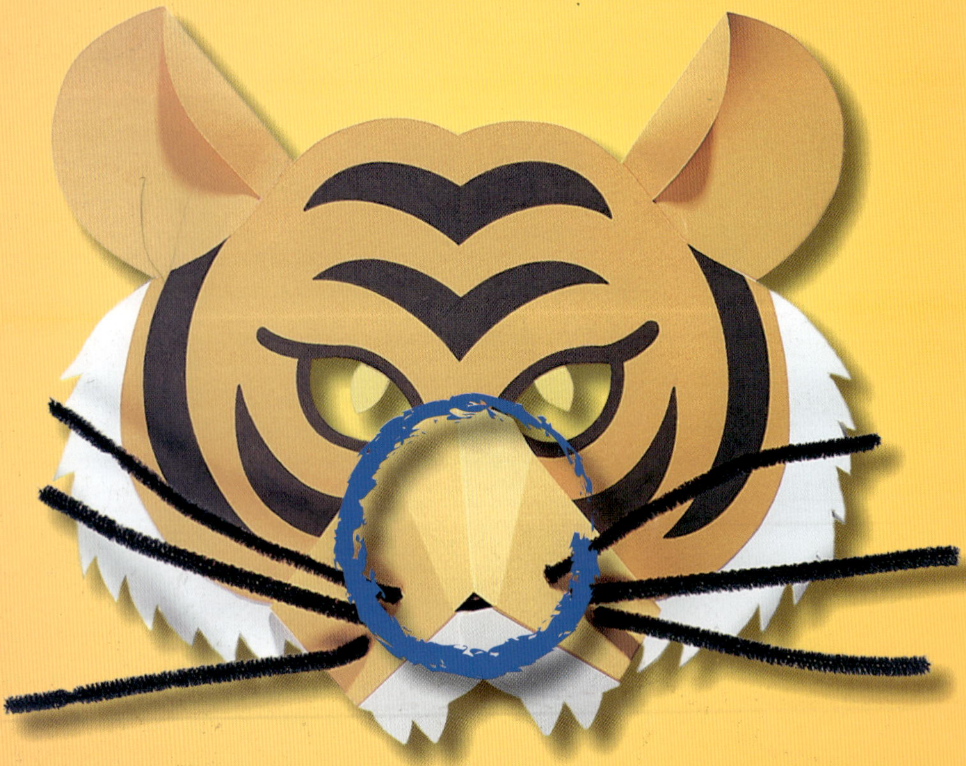

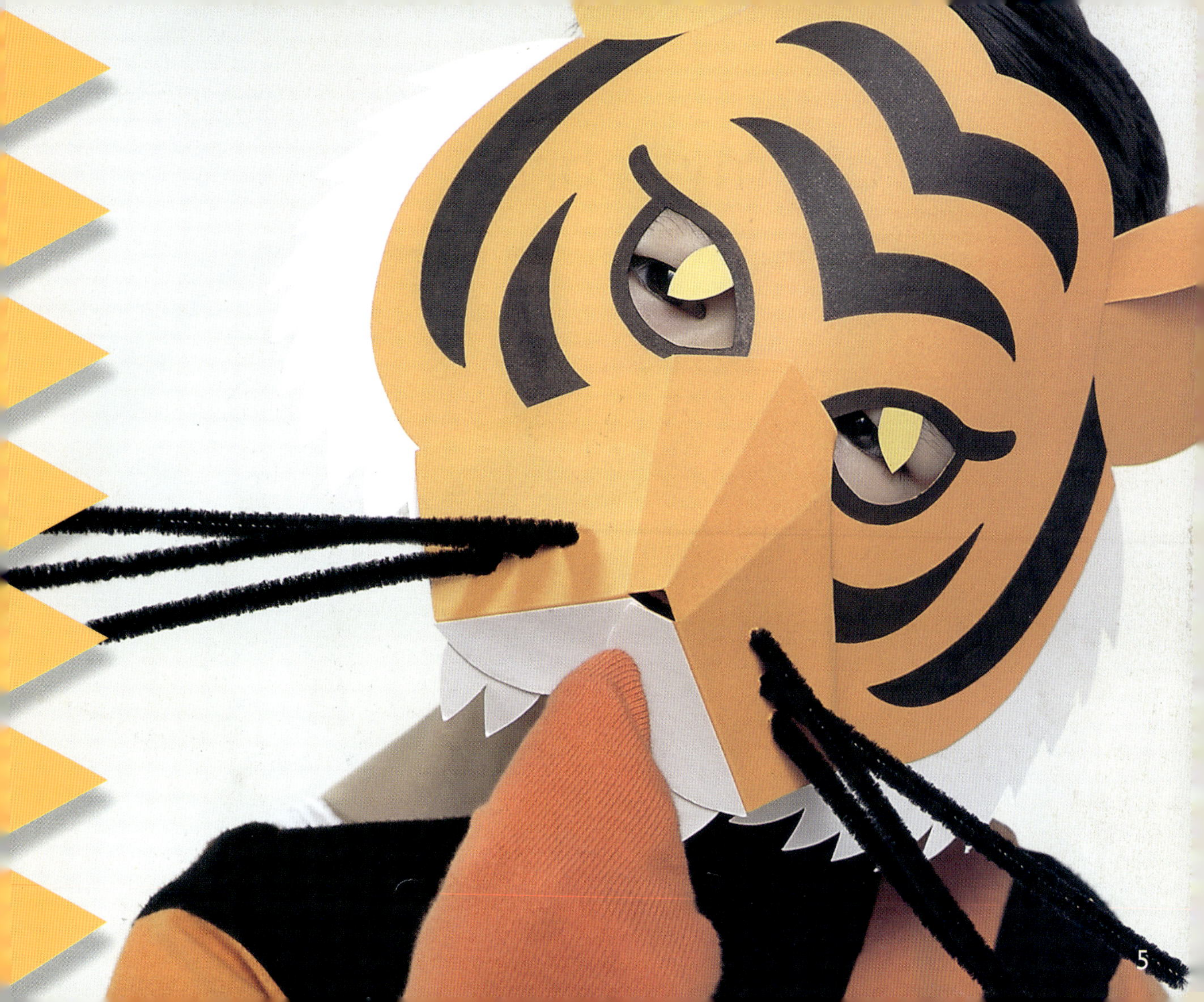

Look at my ears.

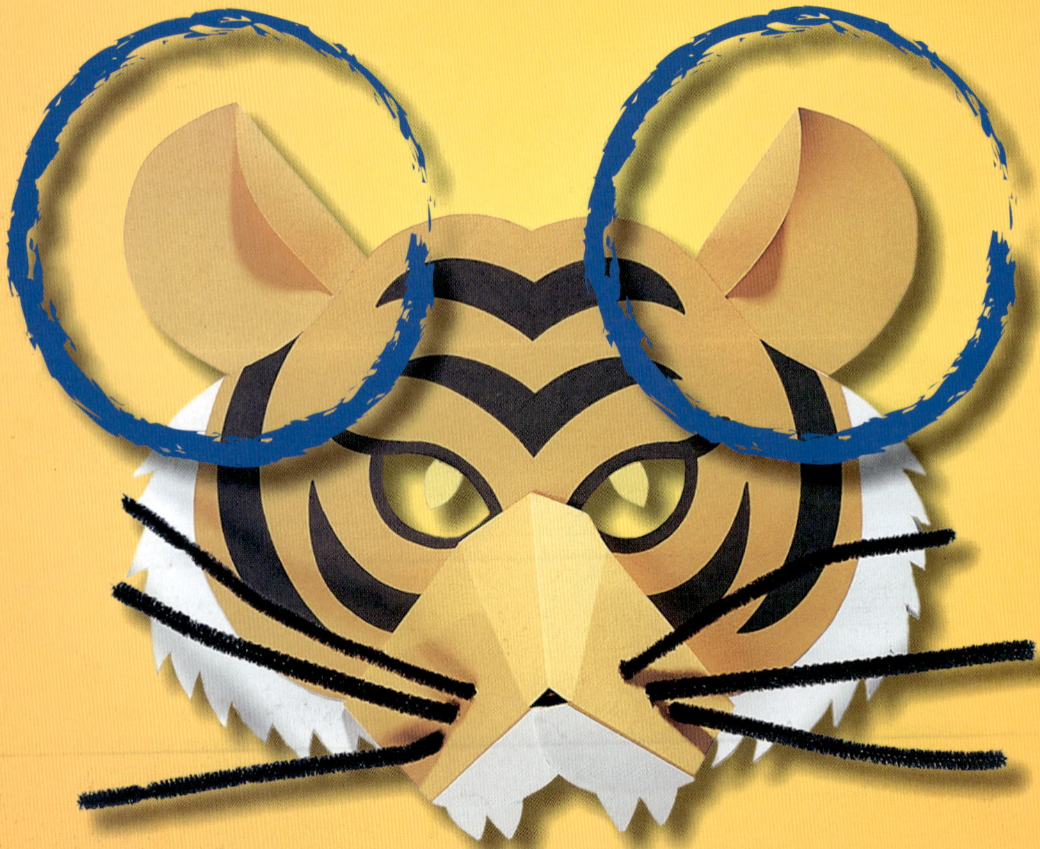

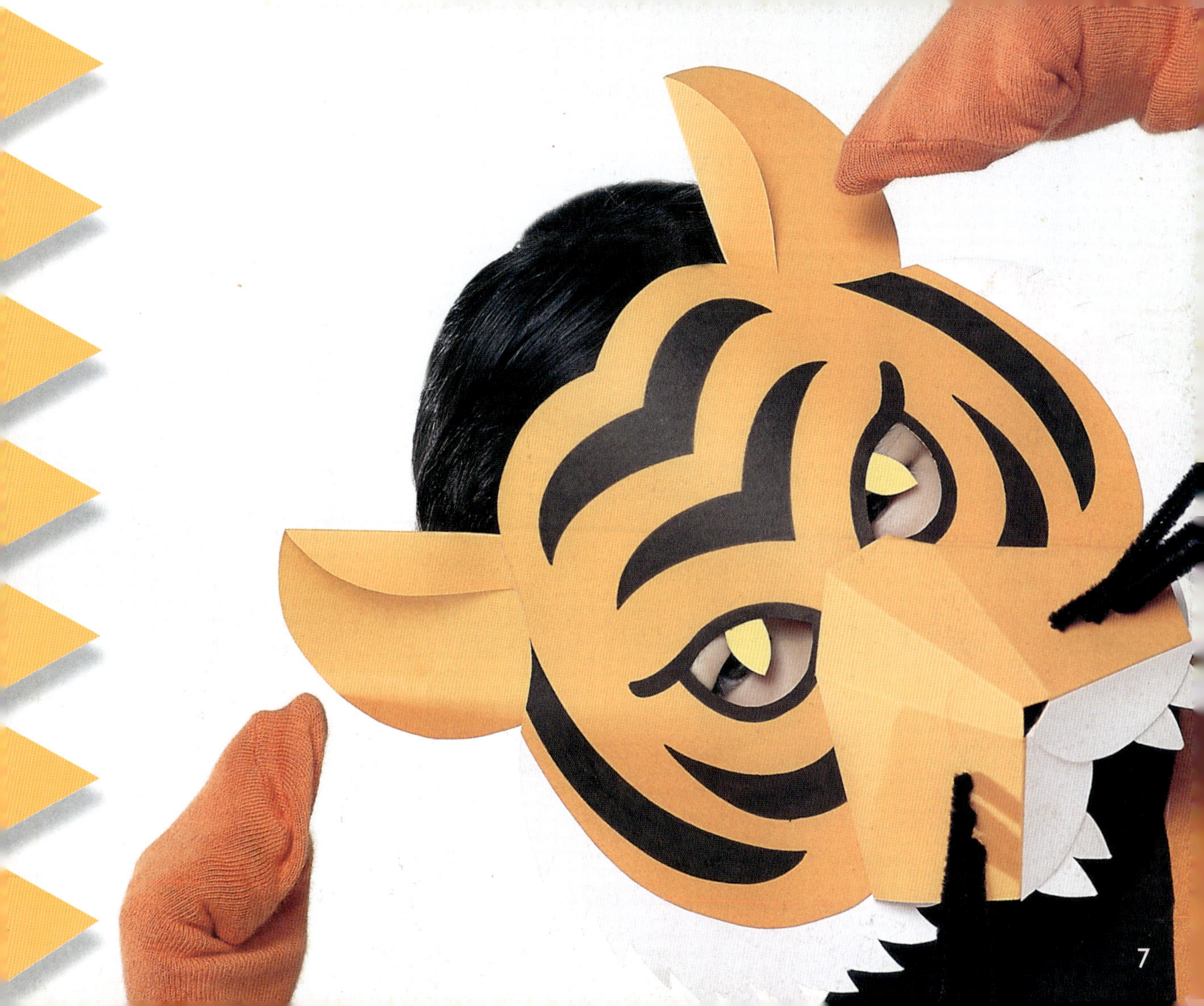

Look at my whiskers.

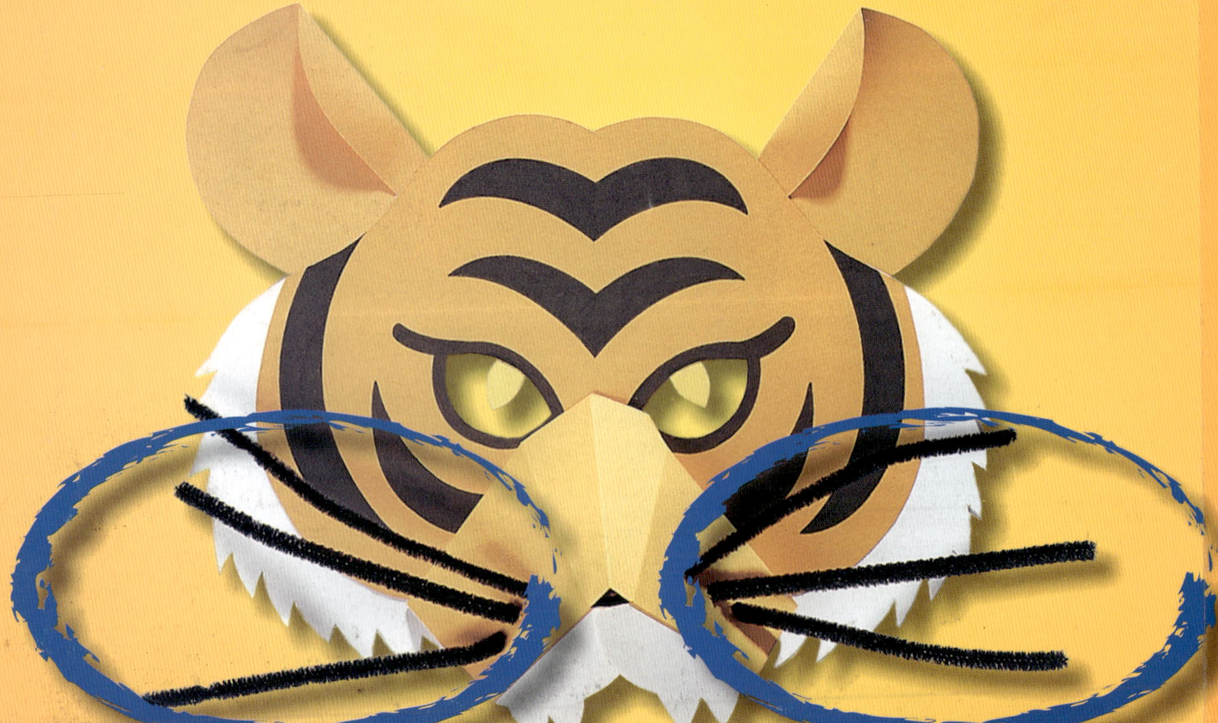

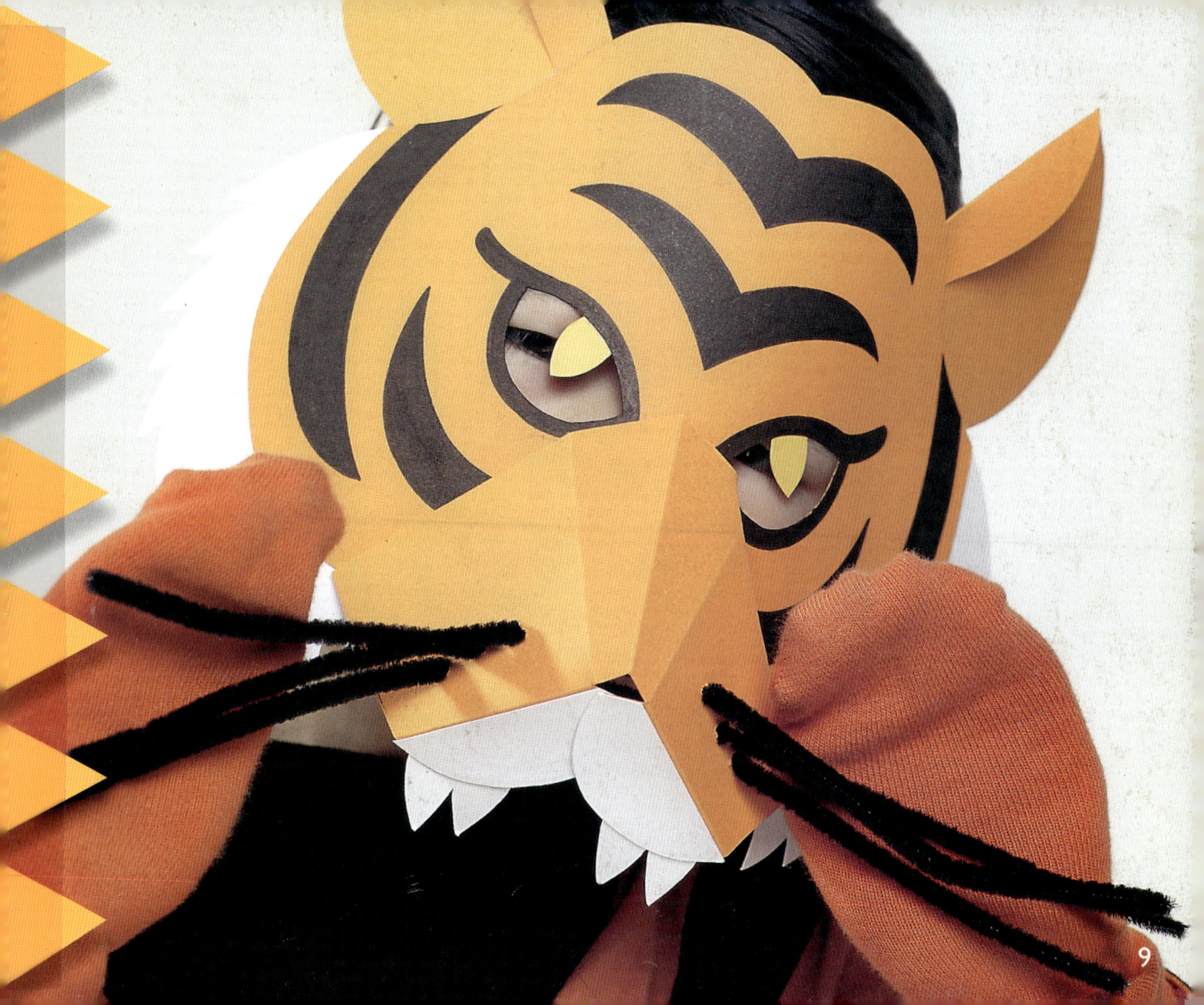

Look at my teeth.

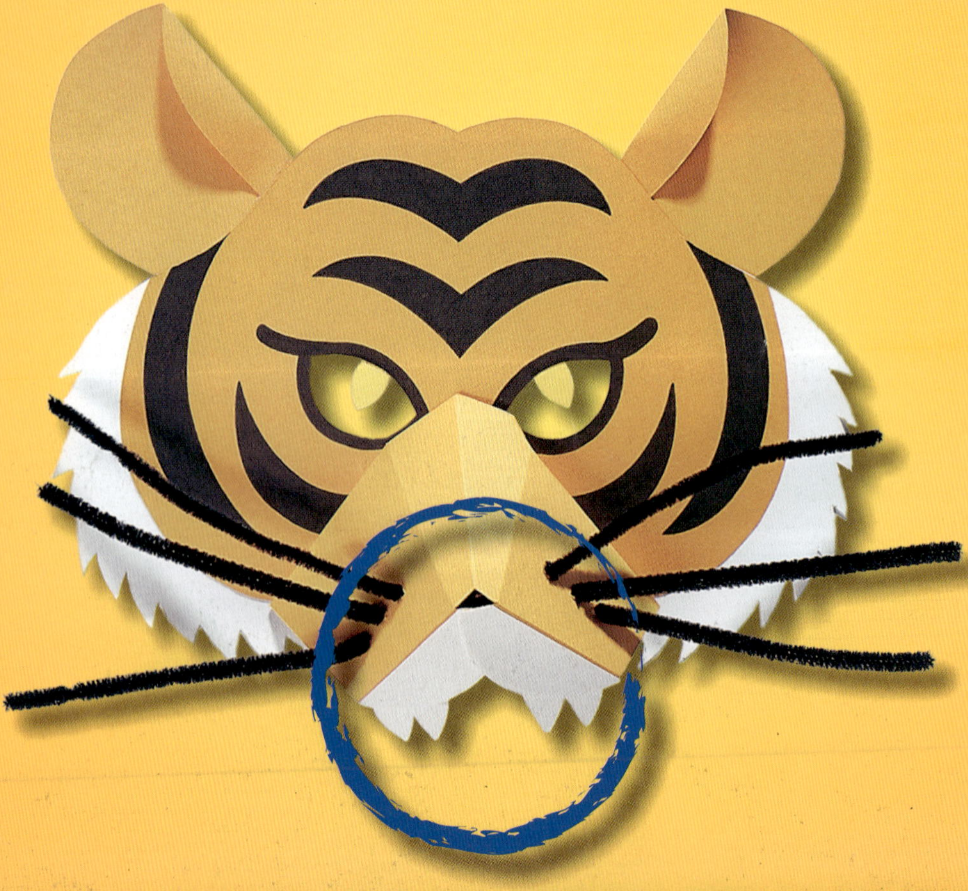

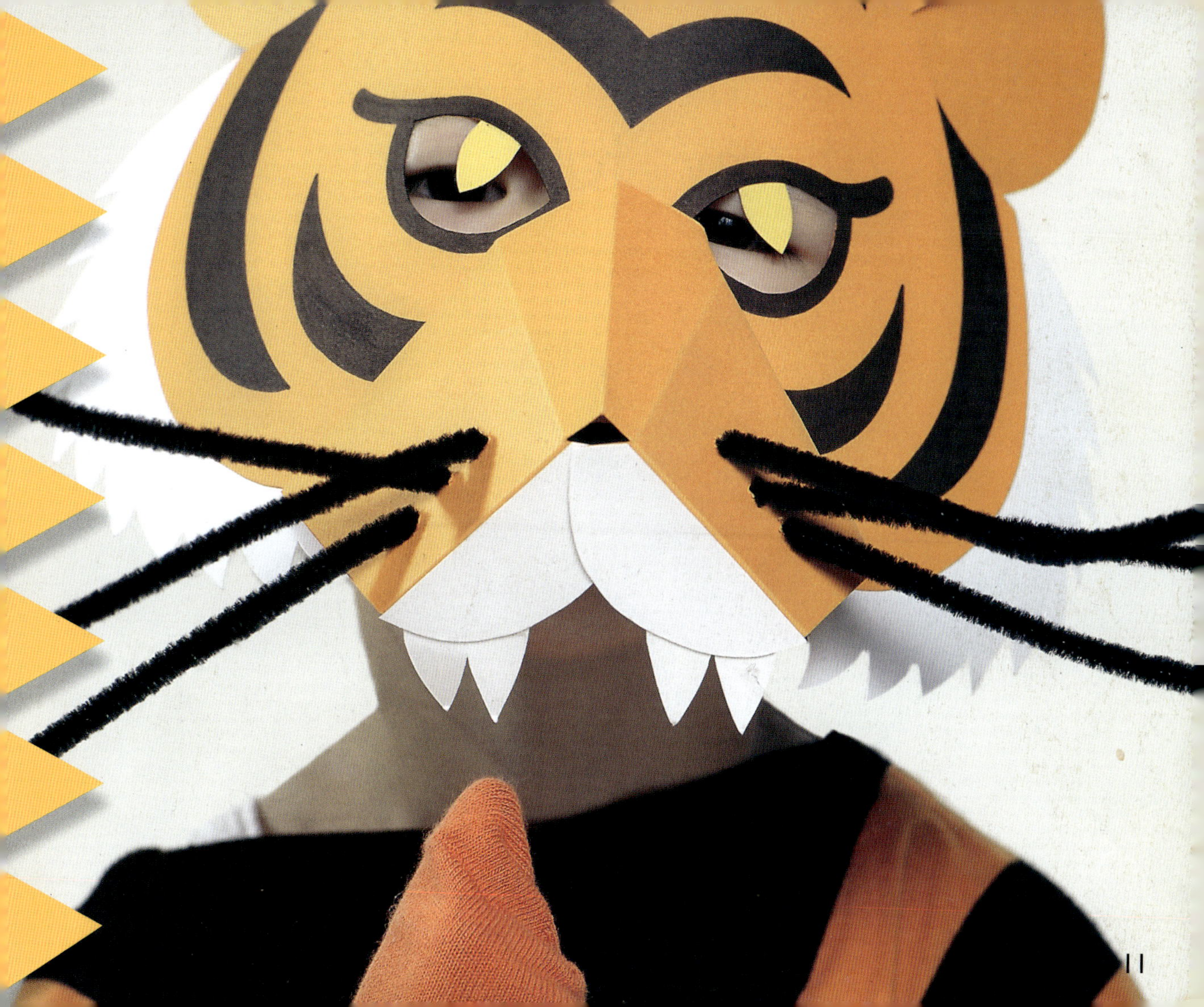

Look at my tail.

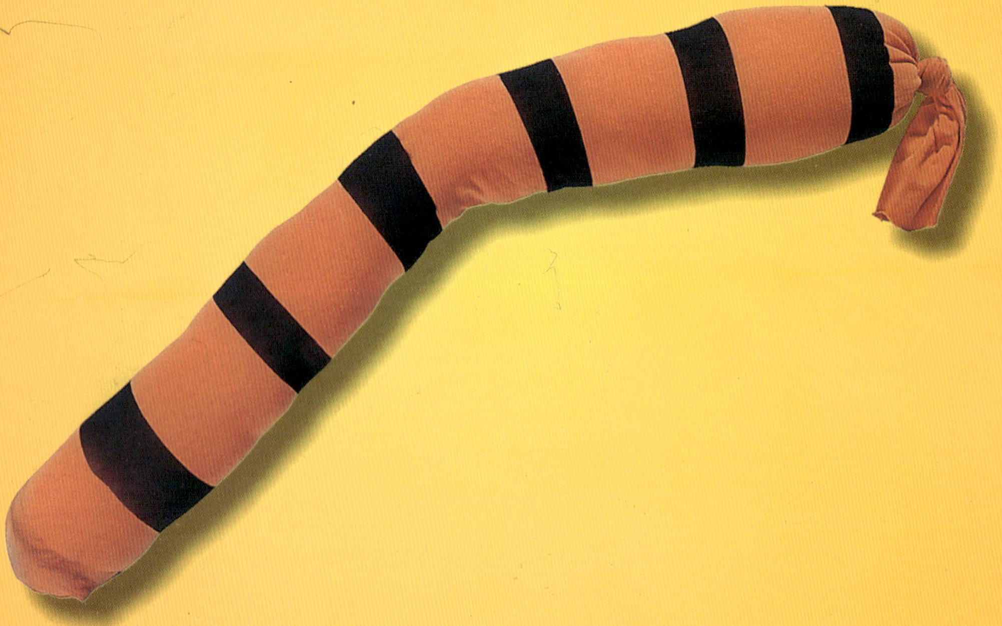

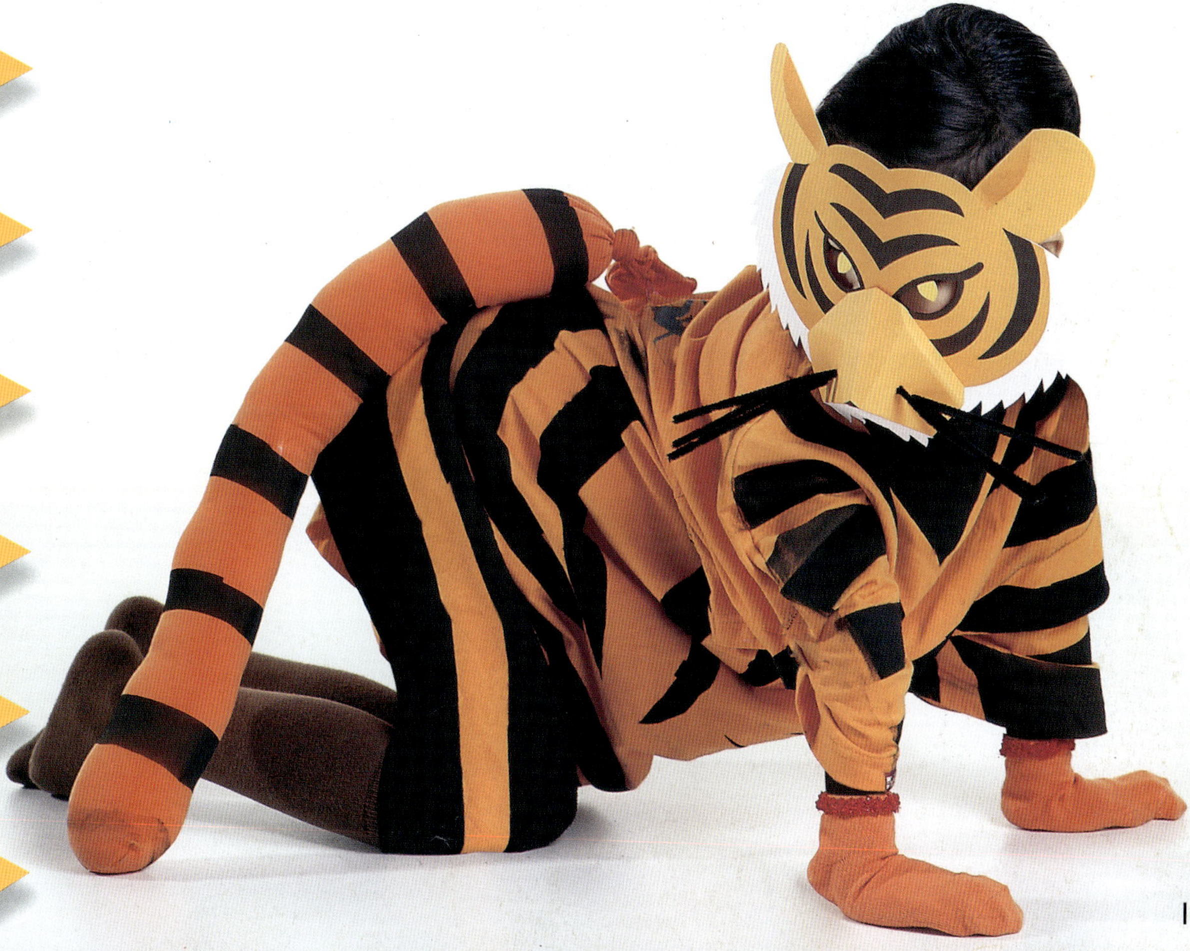

Look at my stripes.

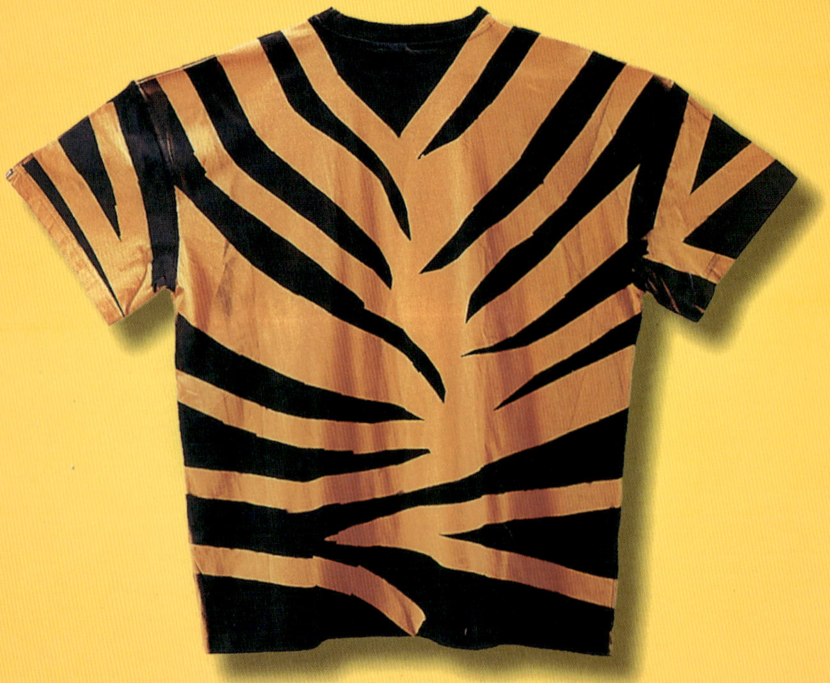

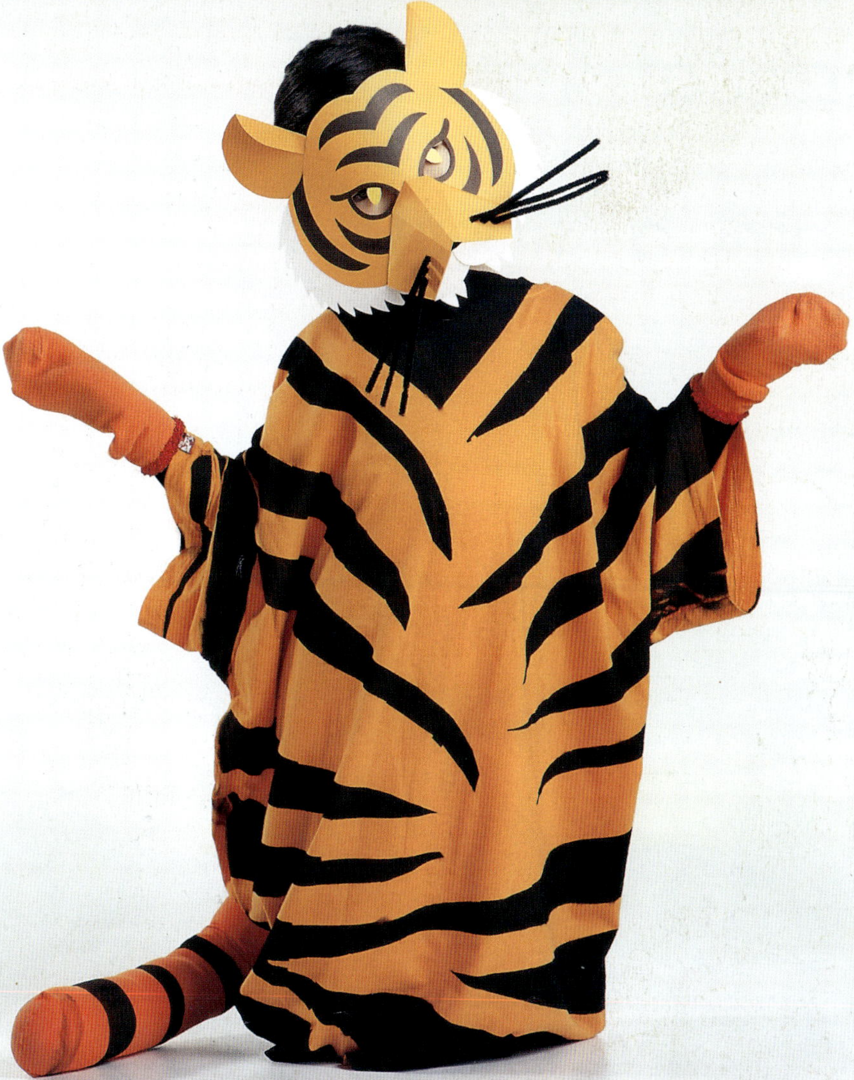

Look at me.

I am a tiger!

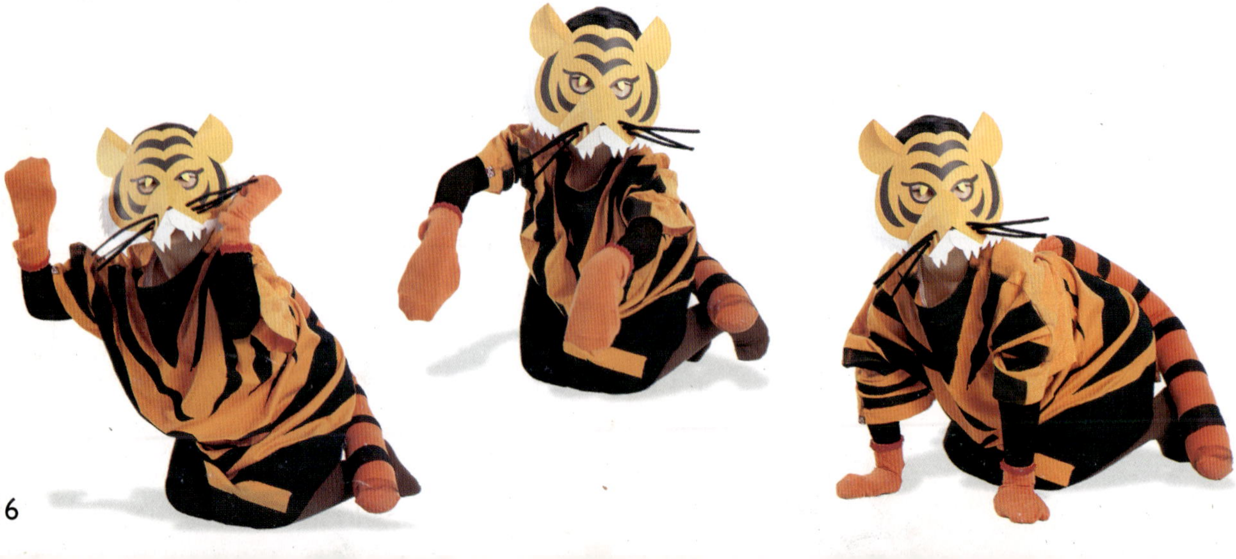